Clifford's
Big Adventures

Norman Bridwell

SCHOLASTIC INC.

New York Toronto London Auckland Sydney Mexico City New Delhi Hong Kong

Clifford
at the Circus

For Joanne and Thomas Sneed

I'm Emily Elizabeth,
and I have a dog named Clifford.
We saw a sign that said
the circus was in town.
A smaller sign said the
circus needed help.

We always wanted to join a circus.
We ran there as fast as Clifford could run.

The owner said everything was going wrong.
He didn't think they could put on the show.

I told him Clifford and I would help him.
He didn't think a girl and her dog
could be much help.
But I said, "The show must go on."

The first problem was the lions and tigers.
They wouldn't obey the animal trainer.

Clifford gave them a command.

They listened to Clifford.
After that the animal trainer didn't have to worry anymore.

Some clowns had quit the circus.
The other clowns needed help with their act.
I was sure Clifford could help.

Clifford tried on some costumes.
He found one he liked and joined the act.
Clifford enjoyed being a clown.

He wagged his tail.
That made the act even better.

The tightrope walker had a sprained ankle.
Clifford tried to walk the tightrope.
He was pretty good.

It wasn't his fault that
he couldn't get off the ground.

Before the next act we walked out on the midway.
Clifford loves cotton candy. He sniffed it.

He sniffed a little too hard.

Licking the cotton candy off his nose
made him thirsty. He took a drink.
The circus man tried to stop him.

THE GREAT
COLARUSSO
LEAP OF DEATH!

It was too late.
Clifford had spoiled the high diver's act.

But he didn't spoil the high diver.
Whew, that was close.

The second half of the circus began
with the elephants on parade.
The biggest elephant had a cold in its nose
and couldn't lead the parade.

So Clifford slipped into an elephant suit
and gave them a hand. I mean a tail.

The next act was the human cannon ball.
She didn't have any gunpowder for her cannon.

So Clifford helped her out.

He helped her right out of the tent.

Then came the grand finale.
I was going up in a balloon
with the circus man.
Everyone came out to watch.

Oh dear, the rope broke. I didn't worry.
I knew Clifford would save us.
He rushed to the rescue.

But he missed the rope. We were blowing away.
Things looked bad.

Clifford didn't give up.
He grabbed an extra tent pole.

He used some telephone wire and took aim.

The balloon was falling like a rock.

We were scared silly.

But Clifford got there in time.
Good old Clifford.

Everybody said it was the most exciting end
a circus ever had.
Clifford saved the show, and me.

Clifford
Visits the Hospital

To Carly, Perry, Griffin, and Tess Elizabeth

The author thanks Manny Campana
for his contributions to this book.

I'm Emily Elizabeth, and this is my dog, Clifford.
When he was a puppy, Clifford went to the hospital.

Clifford wasn't sick. He went accidentally. My grandma
was in the hospital, and Mom made some cookies for her.

Clifford loves cookies. When we weren't looking, he jumped into the basket.

At the hospital, Grandma thanked us for the treat. Then she said she'd like something to read while she munched a cookie.

So Mom and I went down to the gift shop to get
her a magazine.

What a surprise! Grandma loved having Clifford come to visit her, but dogs are not allowed in the hospital.

Suddenly, Grandma heard footsteps. The nurse was coming! What would the nurse do when she saw Clifford?

Luckily, the nurse didn't see him. He was too small.

The nurse had come to check Grandma's pulse and take her temperature.

To Clifford, the thermometer looked like a stick of peppermint candy.

Ugh! That was <u>not</u> candy. It tasted like medicine!

Grandma didn't have a chance to tell the nurse that
a dog had just licked the thermometer. Yuck!

The nurse had to give Grandma a shot. That's when
Clifford decided to leave. He hates needles.

Clifford zigzagged through people's feet
in the busy hallway.

CHILDRENS WARD

He sped around a corner and dashed
through an open door.

The children were amazed to see a small red puppy
in the hospital.

The children had lots of fun playing with Clifford.
Clifford was having fun, too.
And then...

... some girls started to dress him up like a doll.

Clifford couldn't wait to get out of there.

Clifford was in such a hurry, he didn't look where he was going.

What a mess!

One of the children came to the rescue.

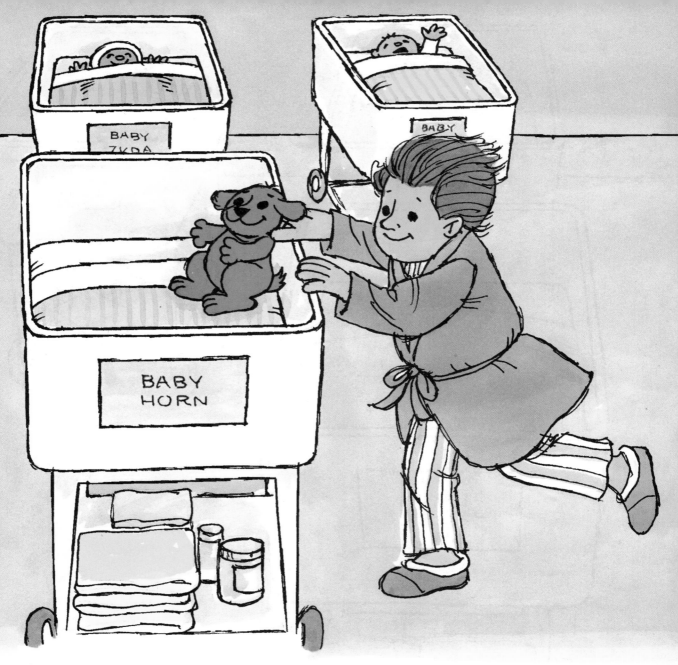

He found a nice, safe place for Clifford.

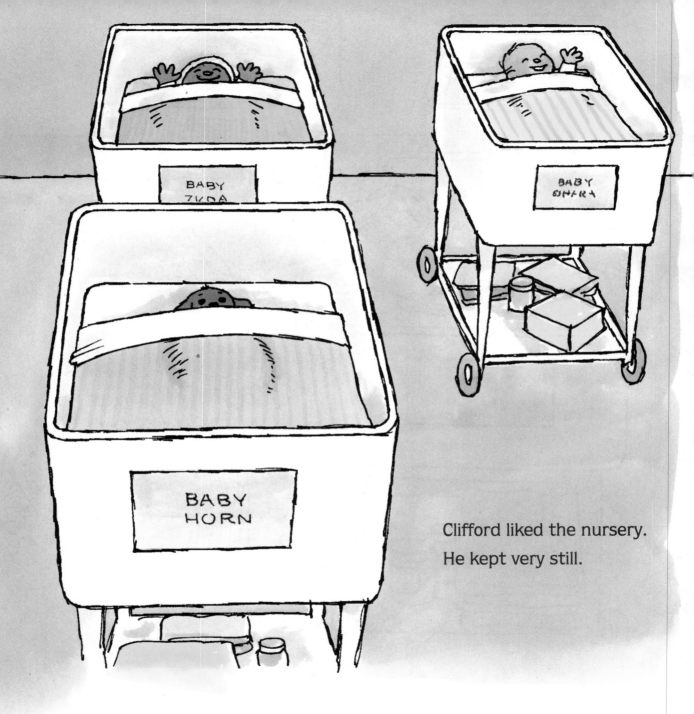

Clifford liked the nursery.
He kept very still.

A proud new father came to the window and asked
to see his beautiful baby. Uh-oh!

NURSERY

NURSERY

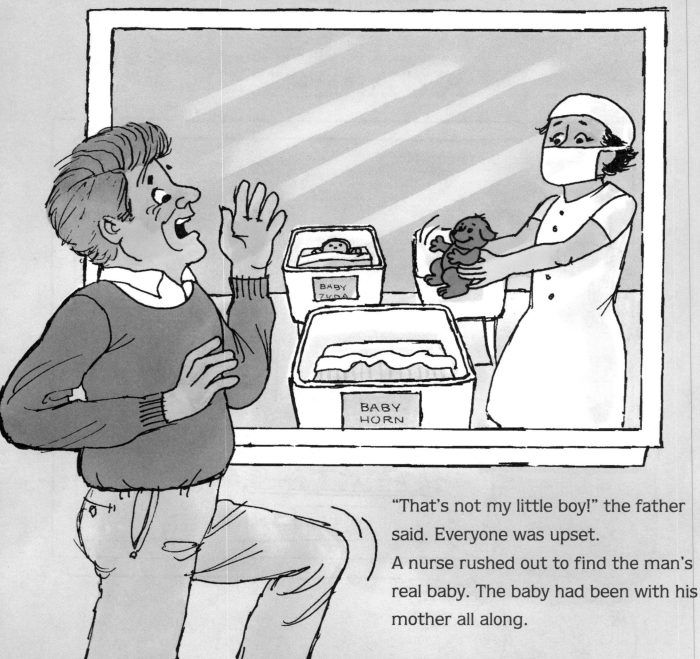

"That's not my little boy!" the father said. Everyone was upset.
A nurse rushed out to find the man's real baby. The baby had been with his mother all along.

Just then, Mom and I came back from the gift shop.
We told the nurse and doctor that we would take
Clifford home right after we said good-bye to Grandma.

Grandma was sorry that Clifford couldn't stay.

But she was happy with the new dog we found for her
in the gift shop. This one wouldn't run away.

Now Clifford goes to the hospital from time to time to visit his friends and make them feel better.

Good old Clifford.

Clifford
Goes to Dog School

To the children of Carlisle Elementary

I'm Emily Elizabeth. This is my dog, Clifford.
Clifford is a very smart dog. He can do tricks.

He can beg.

He can shake hands.

You really should see him play dead.

He's good at that.

I thought he was perfect, but my aunt didn't agree. She was a dog trainer. She said that no dog was perfect unless he had been to dog school, like her dog, Sandy.

Clifford was too big for regular dog school, so my aunt said she would train Clifford herself. First he had to learn to heel. He had to walk next to her on a leash.

That leash was a little too short.

Auntie got a longer leash for Clifford.

That leash was a little too long. Poor Auntie.

Auntie said we would come back to that lesson.
Next she told Clifford to sit. Clifford is very smart.

He sat.

Luckily, Clifford didn't sit down really hard.
The man wasn't hurt—just surprised.

Auntie said that Clifford was pretty good at sitting. Now he needed to learn how to stay. That meant not moving until he was told to move—no matter what happened.

She told him to sit and stay.

Auntie said she had some good books on dog training that I should see.
We went to her house a few blocks away.

She had so many good books about dogs! I love to read.

I guess I was so busy reading I forgot about Clifford.

He was still sitting and staying.

He knew he had to sit, no matter what happened.

Sandy moved, but Clifford stayed.

Even when a Frisbee flew by his nose, he stayed.

And Clifford loves to chase Frisbees.

Even when some dogs and cats played
near him, Clifford stayed. But it was hard.

Back at Auntie's house, I suddenly remembered Clifford. How could I have forgotten my dog?

I ran back to Clifford as fast as I could.

I wasn't very careful. I forgot to look both
ways when I crossed the street.

Clifford saved me!

I guess Clifford will never be the best-trained dog....

But to me, he'll always be the best dog in the world.